Annie Bananie and the Pain Sisters

Leah Komaiko

illustrated by
Abby Carter

A Yearling Book

Published by
Dell Yearling
an imprint of
Random House Children's Books
a division of Random House, Inc.
1540 Broadway
New York, New York 10036

The trademarks Yearling® and Dell® are registered in the U.S. Patent and Trademark Office and in other countries.

Visit us on the Web! www.randomhouse.com/kids

Educators and librarians, for a variety of teaching tools, visit us at
www.randomhouse.com/teachers

ISBN: 0-440-41038-X

Reprinted by arrangement with Delacorte Press

Printed in the United States of America

January 2000

10 9 8 7 6 5 4 3 2 1

CWO

For Jenny Tash, Cool Davy H.,
and in loving memory of my mother,
Dorothy

Chapter

1

"Hear ye, hear ye," Libby Johnson said. "It's time to call the meeting of the Boris Avenue Beauties dog club to order."

"We hear you," Annie Bananie laughed. "What are we going to do today, Madam President? Boris wants to know."

Boris was Annie Bananie's dog. Boris stretched. Then he drooled on Libby's shoe.

Libby wished she had a dog. She was the only one in the club who didn't have a dog of her own. She was also the only one with a grandmother who hated dogs.

Grandma Gert said if she ever saw a dog in their house, she'd flush it down the toilet.

"Meow, Libby," Bonnie Baker said. "Let's not do something boring today."

"Don't worry," Annie Bananie said. "Libby's the president. She always comes up with something good. Right, Libby?"

Libby and Annie Bananie were best friends.

"Right," Libby said, trying to think fast. Today she had forgotten to come up with something good.

"Meow, who wants to see where I almost died?" Bonnie asked. She jumped up off her lawn.

"That's not an unboring enough thing to do at our meeting," Libby said, smiling at Annie Bananie.

"It sure is," Bonnie said. She pranced down the sidewalk, then stopped and jumped up and down on one spot. "It

2

happened right here," she shouted. "Too bad you didn't live here yet, Annie Bananie. You missed my brush with death."

"You broke your arm," Libby said to Bonnie. "Nobody ever died from breaking their arm."

"I didn't just break my arm," Bonnie said, hissing at Libby. "If you knew anything you'd know I had a transverse fracture. The bone broke all the way through and straight across this arm. Remember, Debbie?"

"Oink, do I have to?" Debbie Nash asked as she rode up on her bicycle. "You were doing a double wheelie on my old bike."

"Exactly," Bonnie said, licking her arm like it was a cat's paw. "The doctor said I was lucky I didn't break my neck. If you break your neck, you're dead."

"Wow," Annie Bananie said.

"Fortunately for you guys, I'm a cat," Bonnie said. "And cats have nine lives."

"Oink," Debbie said. "I wonder how many lives pigs get to live."

"Neigh," Nina Blaskewitz said as she trotted up to meet them. "I bet it's more times than a horse. A horse only has one life. I'm too young to die."

"Can we please start the meeting?" Libby asked. "Everybody dies sometime. It's not that big a deal."

"Meow, you're just jealous because you've never had anything really horrible happen to you," Bonnie said to Libby.

"Yes I have," Libby said.

"Name one," Bonnie said.

Libby tried to think fast, but the only really horrible time she could think of was right now.

"I told you," Bonnie said to Libby. "I say for today's meeting we should examine my arm where it broke."

"Neigh," Nina said. "We already did that."

"But Annie Bananie didn't get to. Go on, Annie," Bonnie said, sticking out her arm. "Touch it. Believe me, if you've lived through a major fracture everything else feels like a tickle."

"I know what you mean," Annie Bananie said. She touched Bonnie's arm. "I had to have an operation. Who wants to touch my scar?"

"What scar?" Libby asked.

"On my stomach," Annie Bananie said. "It's from my appendix. It erupted."

"Oink, my gosh," Debbie said. "You mean like a volcano?"

"Worse," Annie said proudly.

"I feel sick," Libby mumbled. "What's your appendix?"

"It's a little piece inside your body just below your stomach on your right side," Annie said.

"You're missing a body part?" **Nina** asked Annie Bananie.

"Meow, what's the big deal, **Nina?**" Bonnie said. "You're missing a body **part,** too. Your brain."

"Very funny, Bonnie," Nina **said,** frowning.

Annie Bananie grabbed Boris's **leash** and started to run. "Here's how it **hap-** pened," she called. "Boris and I **were** running hard. And then suddenly, *yeow!*" Annie Bananie grabbed her side and **fell** down on the grass. *"Yeow!"*

Boris barked. His bark was huge.

"It's okay, Boris," Annie Bananie **said.** "The ambulance isn't coming this time."

"You went in an ambulance?" **Debbie** asked. "Bonnie just went in her **mother's** car. And it was only to the doctor's **of-** fice."

"Hey, wait a minute," Bonnie said **to** Annie Bananie. "How do we know **you** really have a scar? How do I know you're not making this whole thing up just because I said I broke my arm?''

"I'll show you," Annie Bananie said. She was wearing a jumpsuit. She started to take it off.

"Neigh, Annie Bananie," Nina said. "Don't get naked right here in public!"

"There's a scar there, Bonnie. I've seen it," Libby said, even though she hadn't known that Annie Bananie had a scar. "I'm the president. Believe me. Besides, we have to start our meeting before it gets too late."

"I'll trust you for now," Bonnie said to Annie Bananie. "But don't wear a jumpsuit tomorrow."

"Don't worry, I won't," Annie Bananie said. "I'll show you. I'll show everybody at school."

"Hey, I've got an idea," Bonnie said. "You bring your scar and I'll bring my cast and we'll both show everybody. We can be the Pain Sisters."

"Okay," Annie Bananie said in her most excited voice.

"Meow, let's go to my house now, Pain Sister," Bonnie said. "We'll rehearse."

"But what about me?" Libby asked.

"You can still be president of this old club, but you don't qualify to be a Pain Sister," Bonnie said to Libby. "Besides, you already saw the scar. Nina and Debbie can wait until tomorrow. They've never even had chicken pox."

"Come on, Libby," Annie Bananie said. "It's okay if you come with us."

"Gee, thanks," Libby said. But Annie Bananie didn't hear Libby. She and Boris were running to Bonnie's.

Chapter

2

That night Libby was in the backseat of their car next to her brother, Carl. Mr. Johnson was driving. They were coming home from the store. Libby's grandma Gert was in the front passenger seat.

Libby was worrying about school the next day. Annie Bananie and Bonnie would be the Pain Sisters. Libby would be president of a club nobody cared about and have a body nothing bad ever happened to. Libby had to think of something fast. She did not want to go to school.

"Do you feel okay, Cookie Pie?" Mr.

Johnson asked Libby. "You sure are quiet tonight."

"*Yeow!*" Libby suddenly cried out.

"*Carl,*" Mr. Johnson said.

"What?" Carl asked. "I didn't touch her."

"*Yeoww!*" Libby cried louder.

"What's the matter, Cookie Pie?" Mr. Johnson asked Libby. He drove the car over to the side of the road.

"Aggh," Grandma Gert said. "Why are we stopping?" Grandma Gert was partly deaf. Nobody knew from one minute to the next what Grandma Gert could hear. Right now she couldn't hear a thing.

"It's my side," Libby whined. "I'm having an appendix-ache. I think you should take me to the hospital."

"Show me which side hurts," Mr. Johnson said to Libby.

"Right here," Libby said, pointing.

"You're all right," Mr. Johnson said.

"That's your left side. Your appendix is on your right side."

"But it hurts over here, too," Libby said, moving her hand. "I was holding the other side by mistake."

"Aggh," Grandma Gert said. She looked Libby right in the eye. "What's the matter with you?" Libby couldn't look at Grandma Gert.

"You probably just have a little gas, Cookie," Mr. Johnson said.

"Gas!" Carl called out. "Quick, Grandma, open the window!"

"What did you say?" Grandma Gert asked.

"Yeoww!" Libby yelled when the car drove into their driveway.

"Come on, Carl. Let's help Libby walk into the house," Mr. Johnson said.

"What for?" Carl asked. "She's faking!"

"You don't know what it's like to have

knife-stabbing pain, Carl," Libby said. She limped into the house.

"I'll call the doctor," Mrs. Johnson said when she saw Libby.

"Don't get hysterical," Grandma Gert said.

"Remember the night this happened to Dad?" Mr. Johnson asked Grandma Gert.

"What happened to Grandpa?" Libby asked.

"Aggh," Grandma Gert said.

Grandma Gert got a thermometer. She put it under Libby's tongue.

"Follow me," Grandma Gert said to Libby. Grandma Gert and Libby walked down the hallway to Grandma Gert's bedroom. Grandma Gert closed her door. Then she opened her dresser and took out a plastic jar.

"I want to show you something you've never seen before," she said. "Do you still feel pain?"

"Annie Bananie had her appendix taken out," Libby said with the thermometer in her mouth. "She's got a scar. Maybe that's what I have."

"Keep your mouth closed," Grandma Gert said to Libby. "Is that what this is all about? I wouldn't wish appendix pain on a dog. Believe me, it's good not to have anything bad happen to you."

Libby looked at Grandma Gert. Grandma Gert didn't understand anything.

"I know plenty about pain," Grandma Gert said, holding up the plastic jar. "And so did your grandpa."

"What's in there?" Libby mumbled.

"Gallstones," Grandma Gert said. "They belonged to your grandpa Larry. They came out of his body. He had to have an operation to take them out. You've never seen so much pain. These are the gallstones right here in this jar.

You and your grandpa had a lot in common." Grandma Gert smiled. "More than you know."

Grandma Gert opened the plastic jar and poured the stones carefully into her hand. The stones were dark and tiny.

"I feel sick," Libby said, trying not to look at the stones. She could see a sticker on the jar with L. JOHNSON written on it.

"When your grandpa had the operation," Grandma Gert said, "he made the doctors promise he could keep his gallstones. They put them in this hospital jar. Your grandpa kept them in there. After he died, many years later, I never threw the stones away. I guess they're the closest thing I have to your grandpa. That's all that's left of him. Do you think I'm crazy?"

Libby tried to say no. It came out a mumble.

"Well, your father and mother would if

they knew I still had these things. They think I got rid of the jar a long time ago. So let's keep this our little secret, okay?"

"Okay," Libby said, nodding.

"The hospital won't let a person keep parts they take out of your body now like they did back then," Grandma Gert said.

Grandma Gert took the thermometer from Libby's mouth. "Well, you are a little above normal," she said as she read the thermometer.

"I told you something's wrong with me," Libby said, trying not to smile. "Are gallstones as bad a pain as an appendix? Maybe I better not go to school tomorrow."

"Aggh," Grandma Gert said.

Libby watched Grandma Gert put the jar back in its hiding place. Then Libby had an idea. It was the best idea she'd ever had in her life.

Chapter

3

The next morning Annie Bananie came to pick Libby up for school. Libby sat up in bed and listened.

"I'm sorry, Annie Bananie," Libby heard her mother say. "Libby's not going to school today."

"Is she sick?" Annie Bananie asked. "What does she have?"

"We don't know," Mrs. Johnson said. "But she sure was in a lot of pain last night."

Libby felt happy. Her mother had said the perfect thing. Libby listened to Annie Bananie leaving. Then she read. When she got tired, she filled three pages in her drawing book with pictures of dogs and gallstones.

Mrs. Johnson came into Libby's room. "I called the school and left a message for Mrs. Liebling," Mrs. Johnson said. Mrs. Liebling was the best teacher Libby had ever had.

"Now I have to go to the grocery store. Grandma Gert will be here with you."

"Aggh," Grandma Gert said. "Did I hear *store*? I'd like to go and pick out a few nice potatoes."

"Why don't you both go?" Libby asked, trying not to sound excited. "I've stayed alone before."

"I don't want to leave you here when you're sick," Mrs. Johnson said.

"I'm not dying or anything," Libby said. "It doesn't even hurt right now."

"I don't know, Cookie."

"Aggh," Grandma Gert said to Libby's mother. "Come on. Let's go. Libby will be okay. I'll go get the baby. We'll be back in fifteen minutes."

"All right," Mrs. Johnson said. "I'll call you from the store, Cookie. But stay in bed except to answer the phone. Okay?"

"Don't worry," Libby said. "I will."

Libby listened to her mother's car backing out of the driveway. Then she jumped out of bed and ran into Grandma Gert's room. She opened Grandma Gert's dresser drawer and started looking through it. Finally she saw the plastic jar. L. JOHNSON. Libby's eyes lit up. She was glad she had a lot in common with Grandpa Larry.

Bonnie and Annie Bananie could be the Pain Sisters today, but tomorrow Libby would be the Queen of Pain. She would have the gallstones to prove it. She decided she would tell everybody the reason she wasn't at school today was because she had to have a gallstone operation. She would let them see the genuine jar from the hospital with her name printed on it. L. JOHNSON. She thought maybe it would seem more real if she was absent tomorrow, too.

Just then the telephone rang. Libby picked up the jar and ran with it into the kitchen.

"Don't worry, I'm not dead, Mommy," she said into the phone.

"Well, that's good news, cowgirl," a voice said, laughing on the other end. It was Libby's teacher, Mrs. Liebling.

"I was just calling to see how you're feeling," Mrs. Liebling said. "You sound pretty good."

"I guess," Libby said weakly.

"Will you be well enough to come back tomorrow?" Mrs. Liebling asked.

"I guess," Libby said.

"I sure hope so," Mrs. Liebling said. "I know it's not much fun being sick, and it's not the same when you're not here."

"Okay," Libby said. "I'll be there tomorrow." She hung up the phone.

Libby's heart was beating fast. Now she had to go back to school tomorrow. She decided not to worry. Her plan would still work. She ran to Grandma Gert's room and carefully put the plastic jar in its hiding place. Tomorrow before school, she would come back and get it.

Libby ran to bed. Everything was in place for her to be the Queen of Pain.

Chapter

4

"Is Libby coming to school today?" Annie Bananie asked Libby's mother at the door the next morning. Libby was sitting at the kitchen table, listening.

"Tell Annie Bananie to go ahead. I have to eat slowly because of what happened to me yesterday," Libby called to her mother.

"Wow! What happened yesterday?" Libby heard Annie ask as she was leaving.

"You're not going to school with Annie Bananie?" Carl asked. "Maybe you really are dying." Carl grabbed a piece of toast off Libby's plate.

Libby sipped her orange juice slowly. She looked down the hallway for Grandma Gert to come out of her bedroom. Grandma Gert never stayed in her room this late. Finally she walked into the kitchen whistling. Grandma Gert never whistled.

"Good morning, Grandma," Libby said in her happiest voice. "Are you ready to make some of your nice delicious potatoes?"

Grandma Gert reached for the frying pan. Right now she couldn't hear a thing. Libby sneaked into Grandma Gert's room. She walked quietly across the carpeting, opened the dresser, and got the plastic jar. She slipped the jar into her backpack. She headed fast for the door, not even stopping to close her backpack. She knew she was a thief, but she promised herself she would only be a thief for the day.

"Have a good day, Cookie Pie," Mrs.

Johnson called from the baby's room. "Take it easy, and no running. Okay?"

"Okay," Libby called.

"Aggh, Libby," Grandma Gert called. She followed Libby to the front door. "Do you remember our little secret?"

"Yes," Libby said.

"I realized I can't remember the last time I looked at the stones before the other night," Grandma Gert whispered. "I think Grandpa Larry was trying to give me a sign. He was trying to tell me something. Do you think I'm crazy?"

"Not really," Libby said. "But I don't want to be late to school."

"I have to tell you one more thing," Grandma Gert said. "Do you remember I told you that you and your grandpa had a lot in common?"

"Yes," Libby said.

"I hope you'll forgive me for keeping this a secret from you all these years,"

Grandma Gert said quickly. "But your grandfather loved dogs. His favorite was a collie."

"You mean you let Grandpa Larry have a collie?" Libby asked.

"Aggh, of course not," Grandma Gert said. "He never had a dog during the forty years we were married. You know what I'd do if I ever saw a dog in my house. Now you'd better get going. I can tell you more after school. I'm just going to spend the day with the gallstones."

"You mean in the jar?" Libby asked.

"I'll probably take them out of the jar," Grandma Gert said.

"Can you wait until I come home from school?" Libby asked. "That way we can look at them together."

"Well, I suppose I can wait," Grandma Gert said. "I've waited this long."

"Promise you won't even peek in the drawer until I come home?" Libby said.

"All right, all right." Grandma Gert smiled. "If it means that much to you. I had no idea."

"It does," Libby said. "It means even more to me than having a dog of my own."

Libby hugged Grandma Gert. Then she went outside and down the driveway.

"Aggh, Libby!" Grandma Gert called. "Stop!"

"What?" Libby asked. "What did I do?"

"Close up your backpack," Grandma Gert said. "I put your lunch in there. I don't want it to fall out. It's potato salad."

"It won't," Libby called. Then she ran as fast as she could to school.

Chapter

5

When Libby could see the playground, she walked very slowly, like she was in pain. She could see Annie Bananie's red hair shining in the distance. Everybody was out on the playground. Libby would have just enough time to show them her gallstones. When she got a little closer, she heard Bonnie talking.

"Meow, you all just heard about my brush with death," Bonnie said. "Plus you got to see my cast. Now, for an extra added bonus, I give you Pain Sister Number Two. She didn't almost die, but I think you will find her scar close to terrifying."

"I want to wait," Annie Bananie said to Bonnie.

"You can't," Bonnie said. "The bell's going to ring any minute." Annie Bananie looked around. She saw Libby, and her eyes lit up.

"There you are!" Annie Bananie called. "Okay, I can show my scar now."

"I thought you showed it yesterday," Libby said.

"With you not here?" Annie Bananie asked in her happiest voice. "No way."

Annie Bananie pulled down the waist of her pants a little so everybody could see her stomach.

"Oink, my gosh," Debbie said, giggling.

"That's disgusting," Eddie Armstrong said. Eddie scratched his head, then stacked some dandruff on his finger and licked it.

"Meow, get a life, Snowman," Bonnie said. "You just don't know what it's like to have a little pain."

"I know what it's like to have a big pain, Cat Woman," Eddie said. "And you're it!"

"If you think this is disgusting, Eddie, you should have seen my stomach when they first cut it open," Annie Bananie said.

"I feel sick," Libby mumbled.

"What did they do with your appendix after they took it out?" Sifredo asked. He winked at Annie Bananie. Sifredo always winked at the girls.

"I don't know," Annie Bananie said. "I wanted to keep it, but the hospital wouldn't let me."

"The doctor let me keep my cast," Bonnie said.

"Yeah, but wouldn't it be cool if they

let you keep something as disgusting as a decayed appendix in the comfort of your own home?'' Eddie asked.

''I wish,'' Annie Bananie said.

''Excuse me, but I don't have to wish,'' Libby said, feeling her backpack. ''I wasn't here yesterday because I had to have an operation. I have something disgusting to show you.'' She reached into the backpack. ''If you think you're going to be sick, look the other way.''

Everybody got quiet. Suddenly Libby's face got hot. She felt like she was going to faint.

''What is it?'' Annie Bananie asked. ''What's the matter, Libby? You look scary!''

''They're gone!'' Libby cried out. ''My gallstones! They're not in here!''

''Okay, don't panic!'' Annie Bananie said. ''We'll find them.''

"What are gallstones?" Sifredo asked.

"I think they're something like your kidneys," Debbie said.

"I have to find them," Libby said. "They were in a hospital jar."

"Cool!" Eddie said.

"Here it is," Annie Bananie said, pulling a jar out of the backpack.

"That's potato salad," Libby said. She was trying not to cry.

"Meow, this is too hilarious," Bonnie said to Annie Bananie. "This is your last chance of the century to show your scar, and suddenly Libby is trying to steal the show. Can't you see what she's doing? Don't tell me you believe her, Pain Sister!"

"I believe her," Annie Bananie said. "See how sick Libby looks. Trust me. She had an operation. That's why she wasn't in school yesterday. She almost didn't make it today."

"Do you have a scar yet, Libby?" Debbie asked. "Can I see it?"

Riiiiing! The bell rang.

"Come on, Libby," Annie Bananie said.

"You go," Libby said. "I've got to go back and find the gallstones."

"Let's go, Pain Sister," Bonnie said.

"If I lost the jar I'm going to be killed," Libby said to Annie. "The doctors didn't even want me to take the jar out of the hospital!"

"Wow," Annie Bananie said. "Don't worry. I know exactly what to do. I'll run ahead and tell Mrs. Liebling. You just move slowly. That's what I had to do after I got out of the hospital."

"Okay," Libby said. She walked slowly. Then she remembered. This could be a disaster. "Wait! Don't tell Mrs. Liebling!" Libby called. Then she ran as fast as she could to catch up.

Chapter

6

"Let's saddle up our seats, cowpokes," Mrs. Liebling said to the class. "It's time to get started."

"Can I tell you something important?" Libby whispered to Mrs. Liebling. "Remember when you called my house yesterday?"

"Of course, cowgirl," Mrs. Liebling said, walking Libby to her desk. "I can't tell you how happy I was to find out you're not dead."

"Wow, Bonnie," Annie Bananie said. "See! I told you!"

"Can a person almost die just because

they have stones taken out of their body?"
Bonnie asked Mrs. Liebling.

"I don't know, Bonnie," Mrs. Liebling
said. "Let's take our seats."

"But do you think it's possible?" Bonnie asked again.

"I suppose it is, Bonnie," Mrs.
Liebling said. "What's this all about? Why
do you want to know?"

"Because of Libby's gallstones," Bonnie said.

"Excuse me?" Mrs. Liebling asked.

"Libby brought her gallstones from her
operation yesterday," Nina said. "They
were in a jar, but she lost them."

"Mrs. Liebling, can I explain something?" Bonnie asked. "I brought my cast
to show, and Annie Bananie showed everybody her scar because we are the Pain
Sisters. Now Libby has to almost die, too.
Coincidence? I think not."

"Libby's telling the truth," Annie

Bananie said. "The only reason she brought the real jar with her actual gall-stones was because she thought it would be educational for the whole class."

"Is that true, Libby?" Mrs. Liebling asked.

"Yes," Libby said softly.

"Well, with or without your gall-stones, cowgirl, I'm glad you're back," Mrs. Liebling said. "Are you learning a lot so far today?"

"Yes," Libby said.

"Good," Mrs. Liebling said. "Education is what we're all here for."

"What I want to know is why you swallowed the stones in the first place," Eddie said to Libby. "That was pretty stupid."

"When they cut your stomach in half, doesn't all the blood and guts come out?" Sifredo asked.

"All right, cowpokes," Mrs. Liebling

said. "That's enough. Please take out your math homework and pass it up front."

"But, Mrs. Liebling," Annie said, raising her hand. "Can Libby and I go back and find the jar? If somebody else finds it before school is out, it could be a disaster."

"Sorry," Mrs. Liebling said. "End of subject. The only thing I can do, if you want, Libby, is to call your house. Maybe your mother or grandmother could go look for the jar right now."

"That's okay," Libby said softly. "I can wait until after school."

"Now do you believe me?" Bonnie whispered to Annie Bananie. "I told you she made this whole thing up."

Riiiiing! The bell to go home finally rang at 2:45. Libby jumped up from her desk. This had been the longest day of her life.

"Okay, cowpokes," Mrs. Liebling said. "You can all go home, home on the range. Libby, would you stay after for a moment, please? Everybody else, happy trails."

"Let's go to my house, Pain Sister," Bonnie said to Annie Bananie. "We need to have our meeting."

Libby didn't look at Annie. She didn't look at anybody. She knew everybody was talking about her as they left the room. Libby just looked at the clock. Mrs. Liebling sat at her desk, grading a paper.

"So, Libby?" Mrs. Liebling finally said.

"I'm sorry I told a lie about my operation," Libby said.

"I know you are, cowgirl." Mrs. Liebling smiled. "Do you know why you lied in the first place?"

"Not really," Libby said.

"Well, I could tell by looking at you today that you were really hurting. I don't

think there's anything more painful than telling a lie. That pain spreads and spreads when the lie gets bigger and bigger. It can hurt more than passing a few gallstones or breaking an arm or even having a scar."

"Really?" Libby asked.

"You bet," Mrs. Liebling said.

"The gallstones really are my grandmother's," Libby said. "They mean more to her than anything in the world." Libby was trying not to cry. "That's the truth."

"I bet I can think of something that means more to her than the stones," Mrs. Liebling said. "*You!* But go ahead and find them. Good luck!"

"Are you going to have to tell my grandmother or anybody?" Libby asked.

"No," Mrs. Liebling said. "I don't think that's any of my business. But I will tell you my experience. When I lie, the only thing that makes the pain go away is telling the truth. The longer I lie, the longer I'm in pain. Do you understand?''

''Yes,'' Libby said.

''Good,'' Mrs. Liebling said. ''Happy trails.''

''Happy trails,'' Libby said. Then she ran out of the room.

Chapter

7

When Libby got outside, even the school bus had gone. Nobody was in sight. Suddenly Annie Bananie darted out from behind a tree.

"Yeow," Libby said, jumping. "What are you doing here?"

"I go to school here, remember?" Annie Bananie said in her friendliest voice. "I can tell you those gallstones aren't anywhere on the property. I already checked."

"But how come you didn't go with Bonnie?" Libby asked. "You two are the Pain Sisters."

"I know," Annie said. "But I wanted to help you find those stones. Let's go!"

"Wait!" Libby said. "I have to tell you something. I didn't really have that operation."

Annie Bananie stopped.

"I just made that up," Libby said softly. "I wanted to be a Pain Sister with you and Bonnie. Now you're probably not even my friend. Please don't hate me for life."

"So you mean you didn't really bring your gallstones to school?" Annie asked.

"Not really," Libby said. "But I brought my grandma's."

"You mean there really are gallstones but they actually came out of your grandma Gert?"

"Well, they came out of her dresser," Libby said.

"But you really lost them on the way to school, right?"

"Right," Libby said. "That's the truth. I swear."

"Okay, so you only told a one-half lie," Annie said. "The great news is there are still stones out there somewhere. Don't worry. Follow me, Ms. Hospital Patient. I know exactly what to do. We'll find that jar, and your grandma will never know you lost it."

"She doesn't even know I took it," Libby said, looking down.

"Oh my gosh, no, Libby!" Annie said, laughing. "You mean you're a thief, too? You stole the missing gallstones!"

"It gets worse," Libby said. "Any minute my grandma's going to look for her jar. I don't know what she'll do if she can't find it."

"Quick!" Annie Bananie said. "This is a crisis! I believe you that they didn't take out your gallstones. But are you sure they didn't take out your brain?"

Annie Bananie and Libby ran. They never once stopped looking down for the jar. They spotted a bottle top, an empty yogurt container, and a comb with missing teeth, but no gallstones. Annie Bananie opened the lid of a garbage can.

"I should go home and get Boris," she said. "He'd sniff those stones out."

"We don't have time!" Libby said.

Annie leaned over the side of the can to get a good look.

"It's not in there," Libby said. "Who's going to find something as valuable as that jar and throw it away? Somebody probably already found it and stole it. Like Bonnie."

"If anybody stole it, it wasn't Bonnie," Annie said. "Trust me. She didn't believe a word you said. She wasn't even going to look for the jar."

Annie Bananie and Libby turned the corner onto their street, Barry Avenue.

They saw something on the grass that made them stop dead in their tracks. It was Bonnie.

"I found it! I found it!" Bonnie called, waving a jar in the air. She sprang up and ran toward Libby's house.

"Wait, Pain Sister!" Annie Bananie shouted. "Let me see the stones first."

"Stop, Bonnie!" Libby yelled. "I'll give you a reward!"

"Meow, how much? A million dollars?" Bonnie asked as she handed over the jar. She fell on the ground, laughing.

"That's a peanut butter jar," Libby cried out. "That's not from a hospital."

"Neither was the jar you brought your potato salad in," Bonnie said. "But at least mine has real rocks and not invisible stones."

"How did you do it, Pain Sister?" Annie laughed.

"Simple," Bonnie said. "I ran home

and got the empty jar from my house, and I picked four rocks out of the alley. There's two million out there. Anybody who wanted to be a Pain Sister could do it."

"Well, I didn't," Libby said.

"Believe me," Annie Bananie said to Bonnie. "Libby's not a total liar."

"If Libby's not a total liar I'll give her a reward," Bonnie said.

"What?" Annie Bananie asked.

"Honorary membership in the Pain Sisters," Bonnie said.

"What else?" Annie asked.

"Okay, she can be *president* of the Pain Sisters."

"Cat's honor, Pain Sister?" Annie Bananie asked.

"Cat's honor," Bonnie hissed.

"I don't want to be president of the Pain Sisters," Libby said. "You were right, Bonnie. I don't qualify to be a regular Pain Sister. I wish I never wanted to be one in the first place. What's so great about pain, anyway?"

"Meow, Libby," Bonnie said. "Does the kitty hear a confession?"

"I confess I just told you the truth," Libby said. "I am not a total liar. I've got to go."

"Me too," Annie Bananie said.

"Go where?" Bonnie asked.

"To find the real gallstones," Annie Bananie said. "It's a long story. I'll tell you later."

"Meow, but what about our Pain Sisters meeting? If we go to my house now we can have ice-cream sundaes like you get when they take out your tonsils."

"That's okay," Annie Bananie said. "Want to come with Libby and me and be the Stone Finders? I just made that club up. It's only a one-day club. Nobody's even going to be the president."

"Meow, no thanks." Bonnie pouted. "I'll go get Debbie. She'll want an ice-cream sundae. But since Libby isn't proven innocent, I think it should be my turn to be president of the Boris Avenue Beauties. Besides, Libby, you're still the only one who doesn't have a dog."

"You're right, Bonnie," Libby said. "Starting at the next meeting when I still don't have a dog, you can be the new official president. I'd give all the dogs in the world right now for the gallstones, anyway."

Chapter

8

"The only place left to look is around your house," Annie Bananie said. "I'll go first. You cover me."

"No, wait! I can't," Libby said. "I'm sure I didn't drop it right there. Besides, if anybody sees me I'm dead."

"All right, all right, don't have a gallstone attack," Annie said. "Follow me! I've got a better idea!"

Annie Bananie ran between the houses and into the alley. She got down on her hands and knees and picked through the rocks.

"Exactly how many rocks were there in the jar?" she asked.

"Are you serious?" Libby asked. "Bonnie's trick won't work. My grandma will know the difference between antique gallstones and gravel."

"So do you have any better ideas?" Annie asked. "Do you want to live or don't you?"

"I guess these sort of look like my grandma Gert's," Libby said, picking up four small stones. "But hers were a little darker."

"No problem! We'll color them," Annie Bananie said. She took a black felt-tip pen from her backpack. "We have to do this carefully. The stones are the most important thing."

"I think the jar is more important," Libby said. "Maybe my grandma won't recognize the stones, but she'll remember the jar. It can't say 'chunky peanut butter' on it. It has to be an authentic hospital jar.''

"You're absolutely right," Annie Bananie said. "There's only one place we're ever going to find a jar like that. The hospital."

"What?" Libby said.

"You know, the place where you had your horrible operation," Annie Bananie said, laughing.

"This will never work," Libby said. "There's not enough time."

"The hospital is only three blocks away," Annie Bananie said. "We can't quit now!"

Libby ran down Barry Avenue after Annie. They never once stopped looking on the ground for the jar.

"Are we the Stone Finders or the Stone Finder Sisters?" Libby asked.

"We can be the Stone Finder Sisters," Annie Bananie said. "But first we've got to find the stones."

"Right!" Libby said.

When Libby passed her house, she ran faster than she ever had in her life.

Chapter

9

"Now where do we go?" Libby asked Annie Bananie when they got to the hospital. Annie ran toward an entrance that had a big red sign.

"We can't go in there," Libby called. "That sign says 'Emergency.'"

"I know," Annie Bananie said. "This is an emergency. Isn't it? Follow me. I know how hospitals work."

Libby had never been in a hospital. It smelled like a giant doctor's office. Libby didn't like doctors' offices.

"Let's get out of here," Libby mumbled.

"Can I help you?" the nurse at the desk asked.

"Yes, please," Annie Bananie said in her most polite voice. "Do you have a hospital jar I could have? I had an appendix operation once. I can show you my scar."

"That's okay," the nurse said, smiling. "I suppose I could find some kind of jar for you. Why don't you girls just take a seat?"

"It's really an emergency," Annie Bananie said.

"Somebody will help you as soon as they can," the nurse said. "There are a few people in the waiting room who were here before you."

Annie Bananie stood at the nurse's desk. Libby walked into the waiting room without her. The room was filled with people. Everybody looked sick or un-happy. Libby tried not to look at anyone.

Just then a man in a wheelchair was brought into the room. The man was

holding his head. A baby screamed in his mother's arms. The baby's face was bright red.

Libby knew she would rather be confessing to Grandma Gert than standing in this place. She promised herself that if she could get out of the hospital now, she would never come back again on purpose for the rest of her life. She looked up at the clock. It was three-thirty.

Libby ran out of the waiting room. She passed Annie Bananie at the nurse's desk and ran right out the door.

"Wait!" Annie Bananie called, chasing after Libby. "I told the nurse it was a matter of life and death. She's going to get us the jar in just five more minutes!"

"It's too late," Libby called. "I'm sure my grandma is out looking for me by now. I have to go."

"Without the stones?" Annie Bananie asked.

"It's not going to work, anyway," Libby said. "It's no use."

"But we can still find the real stones," Annie said. "We can offer a reward. Do you want to be a Stone Finder Sister or don't you? Don't you want to end up in any club?"

"Yes," Libby said. "But the gallstones are lost forever. I won't blame you if you hate me for life, but I just want to go home and get this over with."

"Oh," Annie said, looking Libby right in the eye. "You're sure the gallstones were lost in the first place. Right?"

"If you don't believe me, do you want to come with me to my house?" Libby asked.

"And tell your grandma? That's okay. I believe you. Do you really want me to go with you? I'm not afraid."

"That's okay," Libby said. "I have to face this myself. Besides, wouldn't you rather go to Bonnie's? You're still in the Pain Sisters.''

"No I'm not," Annie Bananie said. "I thought it was a stupid idea for a club in the beginning. I'm going to tell Bonnie. At least I'll get an ice-cream sundae. You're the bravest person I know, Libby. Come over after you tell your grandma, if you don't get killed.''

"All right," Libby said.

"Who knows?" Annie said. "Maybe your grandma won't be so mad. They're just gallstones. It's not like you stole her heart or anything.''

"Yes it is," Libby said, trying not to cry. "Trust me.''

Chapter

10

Libby started slowly across the street. Suddenly she saw something that made her run. Grandma Gert was standing out in front of their house.

"Hi, Grandma," Libby called. "You didn't look at the stones yet, did you?"

"Aggh," Grandma Gert said, opening her purse. "What took you so long? I've been waiting. I've got the stones right here." She lifted the plastic jar out of her purse.

"Where did you find that?" Libby asked.

"What do you mean where did I find

it?" Grandma Gert asked. "Well, actually, it was the strangest thing. After you left for school, I went into my room and there it was. Right on the floor. It was as if the jar had jumped out of my dresser drawer and landed on the carpet."

"I can explain everything," Libby said softly.

"Only one thing could possibly have happened," Grandma Gert said. "Your grandpa Larry was trying to give me another sign. He was saying, 'Gert, it's time to let me go.' "

"Are you sure?" Libby asked.

"Of course I'm sure," Grandma Gert said. "You don't think I'm crazy, do you? Keeping a memory of your grandpa's pain is crazy! Besides, you can't keep somebody's body alive in a jar. You have to keep the person alive in your heart. That's exactly where your grandpa is, all right." Grandma Gert pointed to her heart.

Then she put the jar into Libby's hands. "Follow me!" she said.

Libby followed Grandma Gert into the alley. She held the jar tight.

Grandma Gert lifted the lid off a trash bin. Then she took the jar carefully from Libby's hands. "It's time for me to say good-bye," she said.

"No, Grandma!" Libby shouted. "Don't throw Grandpa in the garbage. This is all my fault. I took the jar from your dresser, and it must have dropped out of my backpack before I even left your room. I was only going to borrow it for one day to show my class. This was the worst day of my life. I promise."

Grandma Gert stared at the jar.

"I'm sorry I was a thief," Libby cried. "I'm sorry I made you think Grandpa was giving you a sign."

"Aggh, I'm sorry, too," Grandma Gert said. "But don't cry. I don't blame

you for wanting to show off your grandpa.
I wish he was alive right now to see you.
He'd be proud to see how you've grown
up."

"I have?" Libby asked.

"Of course," Grandma Gert said. "It
takes a grown-up person to tell the truth.
Believe you me."

"Are you going to have to tell my mom
and dad?" Libby asked.

"I'm afraid so," Grandma Gert said.
"I have to tell them the truth about two
things. First, that I hid the gallstones all
these years."

"What's the second thing?" Libby
asked.

"The second thing is I think it's time
for you to have a dog. If it's okay with
them, it's okay with me."

"Excuse me?" Libby said.

"Don't worry, you're not losing your
hearing," Grandma Gert said. "I did say

'dog.' It's what your grandpa would have wanted.''

''What do you mean?'' Libby asked.

''This morning as you were leaving for school you told me you'd rather see Grandpa's gallstones than have a dog. I knew the minute I saw his gallstone jar on my floor that your grandpa was giving me another sign. He was saying, 'Gert, listen to me. Life is short. At least let Libby have a dog.' You don't think I'm crazy, do you?''

''Of course not, Grandma,'' Libby said. ''But are you sure that was still a sign, since I lied?''

''You didn't tell the truth, but I know your grandpa. He always had a funny way of getting me to see things. He was giving me a sign, all right.'' Grandma Gert laughed.

''Grandma, are you sure you feel okay?''

"Okay?" Grandma Gert laughed again. "This is the best I've felt in years. Now I can get on with my life. If it wasn't for you wanting to be in pain like the Bananie girl, this might never have happened. I have you to thank for that, Libby. Thank you."

"It's okay," Libby said. "I promise I won't ever go into your dresser drawers without asking again."

"I know you won't," Grandma Gert said. She kissed the jar good-bye. Libby kissed the jar too. Then Grandma Gert tossed it gently into the bin.

"Aggh," Grandma Gert said, wiping her eyes.

"If I get a boy dog, do you know what I'm going to name him?" Libby asked. "Larry!"

"Larry," Grandma Gert said, smiling. "That's a nice name. But I'm not walking him. Remember that!"

"I will!" Libby said.

"I don't want a big dog like that Boris monster. I don't want one of those dogs that barks all the time. And he has to be potty trained, or I'll flush him down the toilet."

"He will be," Libby said. "Maybe Larry can be a collie. They're smart!"

"Aggh," Grandma Gert said. "I'd better go start dinner. As soon as your parents come home, I'll tell them."

"This is the best day of my life," Libby said. She hugged Grandma Gert. "I'll be back in ten minutes. Okay?"

"Okay, okay," Grandma Gert said as she walked out of the alley. "I hope I don't go crazy with a dog in the house."

"You won't," Libby said. "I promise." Then she ran all the way to Bonnie's house to tell her and Annie Bananie the news.

Libby's Rules on How to Train Larry (My New DOG) So Grandma Gert Won't Ever Want to Flush Him Down the Toilet

1. Train Larry not to sniff, beg for, or get close to Grandma Gert's potatoes.
2. If Grandma hears me praising Larry, praise Grandma, too. For example, when Larry obeys, say, "You're a good dog, Larry." Then say, "You're a good grandma, Grandma."
3. Teach Larry never to lick Grandma or anyone else on the face in case his tongue has been someplace bad, like the garbage.
4. Don't let Larry play in the garbage.
5. Train Larry not to jump on Grandma. Then Grandma won't jump on Larry.
6. Never, ever invite Boris to come over for a play date with Larry inside the house.
7. Never invite Boris to come over for a play date in the backyard when Grandma is going to be home.
8. Always be prepared to pick up after Larry (and Boris, if he comes over and Annie Bananie forgets).
9. Train Larry how to sit, stay, and come. Then Grandma will see how smart he is.

10. Larry is allowed to sleep on my bed, but never, ever let Larry up on Grandma Gert's bed.
11. If Grandma Gert gets nervous around Larry, put Larry on a leash.
12. Only give Larry treats made especially for dogs. Never give him chocolate or other candy.
13. Train Larry to heel when we go out for a walk.
14. Never let Larry bark early in the morning before Grandma Gert wakes up.
15. Brush Larry to keep his coat shiny and bright.
16. Give Larry a bath as often as my brother, Carl, takes a bath—six times a year. Ha! Ha!
17. If Larry ever gets fleas, give him a special flea bath and flea collar.
18. Never, ever let Larry's fleas jump on Grandma in case she really is allergic to fleas.
19. Let other *nice* friends pet and play with Larry.
20. If Larry ends up being a girl dog and not a boy dog, still name her Larry. Her name will just be short for Larry Ann.